For information about permission to reproduce selections from this book,
please contact permissions@astrapublishinghouse.com.

minedition**US**
An imprint of Astra Books for Young Readers,
a division of Astra Publishing House
astrapublishinghouse.com
Printed in China

ISBN: 978-1-6626-5112-0 (HC)
ISBN: 978-1-6626-5113-7 (eBook)
Library of Congress Control Number: 2021922645

First edition

10 9 8 7 6 5 4 3 2 1

This book was illustrated digitally, and typeset in Tipique.
Design by Sandy Lynn Davis and Amelia Mack

Dad, Don't Miss It!

Qiaoqiao Li

mineditionUS

Dad and I are going on an adventure tomorrow.

When I go to bed, Dad is still working.

Buzz buzz buzz!

Next morning, we get a late start
and rush to the bus station.

Dad's working again . . .

I see a big bird flying across the sky.

Could that be a red fairy
riding on its back?

Dad sees nothing but his work.

It *is* a red fairy, and she's blowing bubbles!

The bus stops at the edge of the forest. Finally, we're here!

Buzz buzz!

Then Dad's phone rings again.

Dad picks a rock to sit on.

He says he won't be long. But I'm not sure.

Luckily, I have the red fairy to play with.

The fairy has lots of friends.

A white deer.

A stone elf.

A couple of tree monsters.

A flower troll.

I'd like Dad to meet them.

He doesn't even look up,
not even when we blow bubbles at him.

We wait patiently.

Then not so patiently.

We try to get Dad's attention.

Dad!

When he finally responds,
all he says is . . .

Rooqaarr!

Yikes!

We roll down the hill and tumble into the lake.

Dad jumps in to save me.

Ha ha ha!

The lake is not very deep.

Dad meets all my new friends.

And our real adventure begins.